P9-CQS-932

An
Irish
HALLOWE'EN

An Irish HALLOWE'EN

By Sarah Kirwan Blazek
Illustrated by James Rice

PELICAN PUBLISHING COMPANY
Gretna 1999

This book is dedicated to my brothers and sisters: Liam, Fintan, Alice, Cormac, Thomas, Bernadette, Brenda, Angus, Malachy, and Marian, and to my son, Beau, and my husband, Frank. Also, I would like to express my appreciation to my editor, Winter C. R. Neil.

Library of Congress Cataloging-in-Publication Data

Blazek, Sarah Kirwan
An Irish Hallowe'en / by Sarah Kirwan Blazek ; illustrated by James Rice.
p. cm.
SUMMARY: When Wise Woman Magee is tricked into nursing a goblin back to health, she only escapes with the help of her children whose costumes frighten the goblins.
ISBN 1-56554-413-7 (alk. paper)
[1. Halloween—Fiction. 2. Ireland—Fiction. 3. Stories in rhyme.] I. Rice, James 1934- ill. II. Title.
PZ8.3.B59727Ir 1999
[E]—DC21

99-18323
CIP

Printed in Korea

Published by Pelican Publishing Company, Inc.
1000 Burmaster Street, Gretna, Louisiana 70053

AN IRISH HALLOWE'EN

Long ages ago,
On an isle all green,
We started a feast
Now called Hallowe'en.

Old *brillauns** and webs
Hang from old castle walls.
Oh, the tales that they tell,
Are ever so tall.

So this is the tale
Of the goblins' strange plan.
On Snap Apple Night,*
Here's how it began.

*rags (pronounced *brillyawns*)
*Hallowe'en

Under a dock* leaf,
Old *Rua** sat still.
The other goblins knew
That he was quite ill.

The *Bean Sidhe** she *caoined,**
From a bough in a tree;
Old Rua looked up
And said, "She's after me."

*buckwheat
*Red (pronounced *Roo-a*)
*Banshee
*wailed (pronounced *keened*)

Then the goblins decided
One thing was for sure—
If they nabbed the Wise Woman,*
She would know a cure.

"We'll have to find her;
We just mustn't fail."
They looked high and low,
Down hill, bog, and dale.

*A woman who uses herbs to cure illness

Meanwhile, back at home,
The eleven at play
Were carving their turnips,
To keep goblins away.

A round timber tub*
Sat there on the hob.*
'Twas in need of some water,
For the children to bob.

*A multipurpose tub
*A shelf by a fireplace

So Maise, their mother,
As straight as you like,
Set off to Mogues* well,
On her worn-out bike.

*A well in County Wexford known for its healing powers

The goblins they spied her;
"We're in luck today,
That's the Wise Woman!
Let's lure her away."

Her hair it was golden;
Her eyes they were bright.
Only *one* shawl* like hers—
They knew they were right!

*A woolen shawl dyed with the colors of her family

As she peddled along,
Sweet music she heard,
The harp and the pipes,
And the song of a bird.

JMRICE

She followed the sound,
Just off the path,
And soon found herself
In a fairy rath.*

She began to grow tired.
She lay down for a nap.
"Hush! Shhh! The Wise Woman
Has fallen into our trap."

*A fort built by fairies or goblins

When she awoke,
There stood the three.
“You’ll come with us now,
Wise Woman Magee.”

They took her away,
Off down the *boreen*,*
To one of the spots
That she'd never seen.

"We've a sick one amongst us
That you'll have to fix.
You're the magician.
You know all the tricks."

*A hilly dirt road

She looked at old Rua.
"I'll do what I can."
And quick as a wink,
She thought of a plan.

"Go gather some shamrocks
And some *ceann abain beag.**
I'll mix them together,
In an earthenware jug."

*A small whitish-purple flower believed
to have healing powers
(pronounced *keown aboin beyug*)

No sooner had they left
Than she fixed up a tray—
Some boiled potatoes
And a *cuppa quare tae*.*

*Irish tea with a shot of whiskey
(pronounced *cup-pa quay-er tay*)

Rua ate and he drank,
And in no time at all,
He was fit as a fiddle,
For the Snap Apple Ball.

Then the goblins returned,
And over one's back
Hung *gorse** and the rest.
Maise's shawl was his sack.

*A shrub

They gazed in amazement,
At Rua dancing away.
"She's full of the magic.
She'll just have to stay."

The children home waiting
Sensed something was wrong.
Their mother had been gone
For what seemed too long.

They dressed in their costumes
For Snap Apple Night.
Their faces soot blackened,
Their long sheets pure white.

Out went the eleven—
'Twas the spookiest scene.
They went out to search;
They found the *boreen*.

They knew when they found her,
For they heard Maise shout,
"You wee little devils,
I'm leaving—I'm out!"

She started out running,
And just for good measure,
Grabbed up a great sack
Of the goblins' rare treasure.

"Stop her!" cried Rua.
"She's taken our prize."
Then they saw all eleven,
In their scary disguise.

"We're no match for the spirits."
They stood frozen in fright.
Mother and children
Were soon out of sight.

JMRICE

There was plenty of time left
To enjoy all the fun.
They bobbed for the apples.
Each took a turn, one by one.

Maise made the *caulcannon**
Barnbrack,* what a feast.
In the loaf sat a ring
And a six-penny piece.

*Cabbage and potatoes mixed together (pronounced *cole-can-nun*)

*Raisin loaf with a ring and six-pence used to tell family fortunes (pronounced *bahrn-brack*)

Soon father came home,
And they sat down to eat.
Then father remarked,
"What's the sack at my feet?"

"Now what's this you've brought me?
What kind of surprise?
This sack sure 'tis movin',
In front of my eyes."